The f
of Glitterstar

The Real-Life Unicorn
from Space

by Andrew D Frenz

illustrated by Clara Frenz

Published in the United States of America.
First Edition

ISBN 979-8-6151-7188-8

Visit us on the web at andrewfrenz.com/Glitterstar

To Clara, my
unicorn-loving daughter

Chapter 1

Clara swirled the food around on her plate. Her mom had made one of her favorite meals, pizza hot dish. But her mind was far away, lost in thought. Her entire family was seated at the table. Clara's little brother, Isaac, was making too much noise. Mom was trying to get Isaac to quiet down and eat, while also trying to get Clara's littlest sister, Emma, to put food in her mouth instead of smearing it all over her face and hair. There was so much going on, but Clara didn't seem to notice any of it.

"Clara… Claaarrraa… CLARA!" All of a sudden, she realized that her dad was talking to her. She snapped out of her daydream. "What?" Clara replied, slightly annoyed at having her thoughts interrupted.

"Why aren't you eating your pizza hot dish?" Dad asked. "I thought this was one of your favorites!"

Clara took a bite. It *was* one of her favorites, and now that her daydream had been interrupted, she remembered that she was actually hungry. She took another bite and responded with a groan, "Daddy… it is!"

"What's on your mind then, baby? Is everything alright?" Dad asked in a slightly concerned voice. He had a habit of referring to her as 'baby' for as long as Clara could remember. This embarrassed her slightly, although she secretly also liked this form of endearment.

"Oh, I'm just thinking about something, that's all," Clara answered.

Mom chimed in, "What is it, sweetie?"

Clara paused, uncertain if she should continue. "Well...," she hesitantly started, "are unicorns... real?"

As soon as the words had left her mouth, her fear was realized. Her brother Isaac blurted out, "No, silly! They aren't real!"

"Daddy!" Clara screeched, throwing her brother a dirty look from across the table, while her brother smirked. In a much softer voice, she added, "Are they real, Daddy?"

Dad was taken back, unsure of how to respond. He glanced at Mom, then back at his daughter, and then back and forth again. "Well, uh, you see...," he stammered.

"Have you ever seen one, honey?" he asked her gently.

"No…" she disappointedly responded.

Dad continued, "There are a lot of animals around the world, but I've never heard of a real-life unicorn." It pained him to say, but he didn't want to give his precious girl the wrong impression.

What happened next took both Mom and Dad by surprise. They had expected tears, but instead Clara started to smile and her eyes sparkled.

Clara exclaimed, "Maybe there are unicorns on other planets!"

"Other planets?" Dad asked.

Clara went on, "Yes! We learned about outer space in school. There are tons of planets super far away. Maybe unicorns are on one of those planets!"

Dad thought it over. This actually did make sense. He knew the universe was enormous – there were billions of planets. He responded, "Well, actually, I suppose you *could* be right. There might be unicorns out there on some planet far away in space."

"I knew it! I knew it!" Clara exclaimed. "See Isaac – unicorns could be real! I knew it!" she proudly declared.

Dad was proud of the connection his daughter had made with space and the possibility of unicorns. Who was he to say that somewhere, far, far away in space, unicorns weren't prancing around and doing whatever unicorns do on some planet out there? But he felt he needed to dampen her excitement just a bit, so he added, "Baby, if there are unicorns somewhere out in space, they are probably so far away that we will never see them."

5

This didn't dampen Clara's spirit in the slightest. She went back to absentmindedly finishing her pizza hot dish while daydreaming about unicorns out on some distant planet.

After dinner, Dad brought out some cookies. Everyone picked one out and munched on it while Dad and Mom cleared the table.

Clara got out her markers and a sheet of paper and started to draw a picture. She loved to draw and color; it was probably one of her most favorite things to do.

Clara easily lost track of time when she was doing art projects, and so was surprised when she heard Mom call out, "Time for bed!"

Clara was almost done with her picture and wanted to finish it before going to bed.

She yelled back, "Just a minute, Mom! I'm almost done with my picture."

"Okay, hurry up, it's getting late and you have school tomorrow!" Mom replied.

Clara focused back on her picture. She carefully added the finishing touches to it. "There," she said to herself, "all done!"

She ran over to a drawer by the kitchen and rummaged through it looking for some tape. She finally found it, tore off a strip, and dropped the tape back in the drawer.

She snatched up her picture and bounded up the stairs to her bedroom that she shared with her little brother. They had bunk beds, and she had the top bunk.

She scampered up the ladder and scanned the wall above her bed for an open space to place the picture. She found just the right spot and stuck the tape to the picture and wall.

The Adventures of Glitterstar

Falling back onto her pillow, she gazed up at her picture and smiled, dreaming of unicorns in outer space among the stars. She pictured them prancing around on a planet that looked like the Moon, bouncing in giant leaps due to the low gravity.

"Clara, come brush your teeth!" Mom called from down the hallway.

"Let me get my jammies on first," Clara responded.

"Hurry up then!" Mom replied.

Clara climbed down her ladder, opened her dresser drawer, and rummaged through her handful of pajama options. "There, unicorns!" she said as she found her favorite pink unicorn jammies.

After putting them on, she went to the bathroom, brushed her teeth, and headed back to her bedroom. At the foot of the ladder, as she lifted her first foot onto the bottom rung, she paused and looked out the window. It was a dark and clear night. And even though they lived in a big city, she could notice several stars shining up in the sky.

A smile came across her face as she thought to herself, *I know you are out there, unicorns, I just know it!*

Chapter 2

The next day after school, Clara ran in the front door, dropped her backpack on the floor, and rushed to her art table. She flipped through her stack of colored paper until she found the perfect shade of light pink. Using a black marker, she began to write.

"Mooooommm!" Clara yelled. "How do you spell astronaut?"

Her mom popped her head around the corner and asked, "Why do you ask, sweetie?"

"I'm writing a letter. Now how do you spell it?" Clara demanded.

"A – S – T – R – O – N – A – U – T, Mom spelled out slowly as Clara wrote each letter down.

A few minutes later, Clara yelled out again, "How do you spell wondering?"

This time, not even bothering to come into the room, Mom called out loudly from the next room over, "W – O – N – D – E – R – I – N – G."

"What about different?" Clara asked, a few minutes later.

"How to spell different?" Mom asked to clarify.

"Yes!" Clara confirmed.

"D – I – F – F – E – R – E – N – T" Mom answered back.

"D – I – F – F what?" Clara yelled.

"D- I – F – F – E – R – E – N – T" Mom said once again.

"Oh, okay!" Clara answered.

Mom poked her head in the room and asked, "Do you need me to spell any other words?" She was used to it. Clara loved to write but still didn't know how to spell very many words so she often asked for help.

"No!" Clara answered as she moved on from writing words to drawing a picture to go along with the letter.

After adding her finishing touches, she went searching in the kitchen drawer for an envelope. She found one, folded her letter and picture up, neatly placed it in the envelope, and then licked the flap to seal it.

She then rummaged some more and found the stamps. She frowned slightly as she couldn't find any more of the pretty flower-style that they used to have. Instead, she settled on a boring flag. After peeling it off, she carefully placed it in the corner of the envelope like she had learned at school.

"Mom!" Clara yelled. "Where are you?"

"I'm up here!" Mom called out from upstairs.

Clara bounded up the stairs excitedly and burst into the room where Mom was folding laundry.

"Can you send this to an astronaut?" she asked?

"Clara," Mom started, "I told you not to touch the stamps."

"But Mommy!" Clara protested. "I need to send this letter to an astronaut."

Mom asked, "Is that what you were making? What for?"

"To see if they have seen a unicorn!" Clara exclaimed.

Mom could see that the letter was already sealed and a stamp had been applied. "Well, alright, I guess. Do you even know an astronaut? We need to know an address," Mom said.

"Look it up on your phone, Mom!" Clara said in a matter of fact manner. "That's how you figure everything out!"

Mom picked up her smartphone from on top of the bed where she had left it. She entered a search for "where to send astronauts letter". Much to her surprise, the top result looked promising!

She tapped on the search result and found herself on a site setup for kids to learn about astronauts. There was even a page built for children to ask questions to astronauts. Much to Mom's surprise, there was also an address for mailing a physical letter.

"Here it is!" she exclaimed. "I didn't think it would be that easy to find."

"Okay, can you write it here?" Clara impatiently asked, pointing to the letter. "Then let's go put it in the mailbox!"

"Just let me finish folding my laundry first. It's a nice day out, we can take a walk to the post office. It will be good for you kids to get some fresh air."

"Hurray!" Clara exclaimed as she jumped into the air with excitement.

"Go find your brother and tell him we are going for a walk."

"Isaaaccc!" Clara shouted as she ran out of the room in search of her brother.

After Mom had finished folding the laundry and written the address on the envelope, she rounded everyone up to get them out the door on a walk to the post office. It was several blocks away, but it was a nice fall day so nobody minded. Clara was skipping along with joy as she kept urging everyone to hurry up just a little bit faster.

As soon as they turned the corner and the post office came into view, Clara exclaimed, "There it is!" as she took off running with Isaac at her heels.

Mom picked up her pace as she did her best to keep up with Clara and Isaac while carrying baby Emma.

Clara reached the mailbox and yelled back to Mom, "This one?"

"Hold on, let me see," Mom responded. She finally caught up and determined that it was the correct mailbox. She pulled down the door and Clara tossed the letter inside.

"When do you think I'll get a response?" Clara immediately asked. "Do you think soon?"

"Honey, it is going to take a while for the letter to be delivered all the way to the space center. You need to be patient," Mom advised. But then she realized that she also better not let her daughter get her hopes up too much. She added, "And I'm sure they get lots of mail. You might not get an answer."

Clara groaned out of slight disappointment. But then she perked up and declared, "I just know they are going to respond!"

As they made their way back, Clara couldn't help but daydream about unicorns and astronauts. She just knew they were out there. She was so excited to hear if the astronauts had seen them. She was certain they must have.

That evening at the dinner table, Mom was telling Dad about their day and how they had taken a walk to the post office to mail a letter to an astronaut.

Dad asked, "Where did you find the address? Is it that one place that does a segment on the news every once in a while?"

"I think it was," Mom answered. "I thought it sounded familiar. I couldn't remember where I had heard of it before."

"What do you mean, Daddy?" Clara asked.

"I'll have to look up when they will be on next," he said. "I've seen astronauts on the news before, broadcasting from the space station. They read questions from kids and answer them from space."

"Cool!" Clara exclaimed. "I want to watch it! Maybe they will answer my question!"

"Maybe," Dad answered. "But don't get your hopes up."

"Oh Daddy, I know." Clara answered.

After dinner was over, Dad checked on his phone to see when the next astronaut broadcast would be. It didn't look like there would be one for another week. Mom wrote a reminder on the refrigerator calendar so they could remember to watch.

For the next several days, Clara could think of nothing but the letter. Every day when she came home from school, the first thing she did was run to the mailbox and check for mail. She scanned it quickly for any letter that was addressed "Clara," but none of the letters ever were.

Mom reminded her that it took a while for letters to travel across the country. But Clara wouldn't give up. Day after day, she kept checking, certain an answer would arrive soon.

She had been so focused on the letter though that she had almost forgotten about the astronaut show live from the space station.

Chapter 3

The day of the next live astronaut show arrived. Clara had completely forgotten about the show, although she still was checking the mail for a letter response.

That evening, Dad came home, checked the calendar on the refrigerator, and announced, "Clara, do you know what is tonight?"

Clara responded, "No, what?"

"The astronaut show is on! After dinner we can watch it and see if they answer your letter!" Dad said.

Clara squealed with excitement. "I can't wait! Can we watch now?!"

"No, it's not on until close to your bedtime. If you get your jammies on and brush your teeth, we can let you stay up late and watch," Dad promised.

"I want to watch too," Isaac insisted.

"If you get your jammies on and brush your teeth, you can watch too," Mom answered.

Both kids chatted excitedly about astronauts as they scarfed down their noodles.

"Maybe the astronauts have seen a unicorn in space!" Clara said.

"Maybe they've seen a *dinosaur* in space!" Isaac countered. Isaac loved dinosaurs

23

almost as much as Clara loved unicorns. "A big T-REX," he added in a deep, scary voice.

"Kids, eat your food so you can get ready in time or nobody is going to be able to watch it," Dad threatened.

Despite their excitement, or perhaps because of it, they ended up taking a long time to clear their plates. They had a little time to play, but before long, Mom called out, "Clara! Isaac! Time to get your jammies on and brush if you want to watch the show!"

"Let's see who can win!" Dad challenged as they both bounded up the stairs. Clara, as usual, picked out a unicorn pair of pajamas. Isaac decided to go with his dinosaur pair, perhaps in hopes that the astronauts had found dinosaurs in space.

After getting changed and brushing their teeth, they raced back downstairs to the TV in the basement where Dad was getting it set to the correct station for the broadcast.

"Did you brush your teeth?" Dad asked.

"Yes!" both Clara and Isaac replied in unison.

"Remember Clara, don't be disappointed if you don't hear anything about unicorns. Astronauts haven't been very far into space. They haven't seen everything. And they might not have gotten your letter yet either."

"Oh, I hope they do!" Clara said, maintaining her excitement.

"Here it is, quiet kids. Mom! Come on down, it's starting up!" Dad called up the stairs to Mom.

"Be right down!" Mom answered as she scooped up Emma and hurried down the stairs to watch.

The whole family had just settled down on the couch when a man on the TV announced, "And now, join us as we go live to outer space. Astronauts on board the space station are broadcasting live to answer your questions about space and what it is like to be an astronaut."

"Welcome, Earth!" an astronaut greeted as he floated, suspended in zero gravity inside the space shuttle. "Thank you for joining us. My name is Astronaut Paul, and I am here to answer your questions. Kids from all over the world have sent in emails and letters. We will choose a few to answer tonight. Sally, do you have a question or two ready for us?"

The camera turned to Sally, another astronaut on board the shuttle. "Thanks Paul! Yes, here is the first question from Louie in California. Louie asks, *How do you sleep in space? Don't you float off your bed?*"

"That's a great question Louie," Paul chuckled. "Yes, if we had a bed like on Earth, we wouldn't stay in it. And our sheets and blankets would float right off of us! On the space station, we sleep in a special sleeping bag that ties us into the wall so we don't float around."

He pushed off the wall to float towards one of the sleeping bags to demonstrate. "See, this way we stay nice and snug! You'd never want to sleep on the wall on Earth, but without gravity, there really isn't any up or down, so it's all the same!"

Paul slipped out of the sleeping bag. As he floated back towards Sally, he asked, "Okay, what question is up next, Sally?"

"Let's see," she answered as she flipped through a stack of papers. "I'll answer this one. Jane from Louisiana wrote, *How do you eat lunch in space? Does the food float off of your plate?*"

Sally continued, "That's a great question Jane! Yes, the food would float away if we tried to eat on a plate like we do on Earth! Instead, most of our food comes in tubes. We squeeze it out into our mouth. We mostly eat food without crumbs because the crumbs would just fly away and get everything messy!"

"What is your favorite food in space?" Paul asked Sally.

"Hmm...," Sally pondered. "I would have to say... peanut butter! Yum!"

"Oh yes, I love peanut butter too!" agreed Paul. "But I also love eating candy that you can toss into the air and catch with your mouth!"

He pulled out a fun size bag of M&Ms, ripped it open, and twirled a red M&M in the air where it floated for a few seconds before he caught it in his mouth and crunched it with a smile.

The camera turned back to Sally as she pulled out a new folder, opened it up, and started paging through the papers.

Sally spoke as she thumbed slowly through the letters. "Alright, I think we only have time for one more question. A shuttle just arrived today to restock our supplies. It happened to also have a new batch of letters. Let's see if we can find a good one."

"Ah-ha," she exclaimed. "Here we go, let's read this one."

She held the letter up to the camera as she read it aloud:

Deer Astronaut,
have you ever seen a
Vinacorn in awter space?

I've ben wondering
if they are real and
I think thae mite live on
a different planit.

from Clara

"Deer Astronaut,

have you ever seen a Uinacorn in awter space?

I've ben wondering if they are real and I think thae mite live on a different planit.

from Clara"

Mom let out a gasp, Dad couldn't contain his excitement and hurriedly whispered, "Clara, Clara, is that your letter? Is that yours?"

"Yes!" squealed Clara with excitement.

"Hush! Shhh!" Mom urged so they could hear how the astronaut would answer. The whole family stared at the screen, holding their breath.

Chapter 4

Sally flashed a quick smile which quickly gave in to a look of deep contemplation.

"Wow," she exclaimed, "I think that is the best question I have ever been asked!"

She paused for a moment before continuing, "I *have* seen a unicorn in space, actually. You can see it too from Earth. There is a constellation called Monoceros. Do you know what a constellation is? It is a collection of stars that, in this case, looks like the outline of a unicorn!"

Clara and her whole family hung on her every word.

Sally continued, "But I suspect you are actually asking about *real* unicorns. I haven't been lucky enough to see a real unicorn in space... yet. We know that unicorns don't live on any of the planets in *our* solar system. But there are billions of other planets beyond ours. We don't have any idea if there is life, including unicorns, out there on any of those other planets. There are so many stars and planets that maybe, just maybe, there are unicorns out there. Wouldn't that be exciting!"

Paul chimed in, "Clara, maybe you will grow up to be an astronaut and can travel to other planets looking for unicorns and other life. We will never know unless we look!"

"And with that, we are going to have to say goodnight folks," Sally said. "We always look forward to spending time with you all back on Earth. Send us your questions for next time. For those of you watching where it is night, go outside and see if you can spot the unicorn constellation. Until next time, keep your feet on the ground, goodnight Earth!"

"Wow, Clara, did you hear that?!" Dad exclaimed. "They read your letter baby. That was amazing!"

"And she said that there might be unicorns on other planets!" Clara gleefully answered.

"I wanted there to be dinosaurs," Isaac grumbled with a frown on his face.

"Can we go outside and look for the unicorn stars, Daddy? Can we?" Clara begged.

"Mommy, what do you think?" Dad asked.

"Well I suppose we can, but it is getting late so make it quick." Mom replied.

"Yippee!" Clara exclaimed as she jumped off the couch to run to the door in the walkout basement that led outside.

Dad got their shoes and they headed out into their backyard to look up at the sky. Dad knew the Big Dipper and the North Star, but that was about it. So, he pulled out his phone and searched for how to find constellations. He discovered an app that he could hold up to the sky and it would show where the various constellations were.

"Let me see, let me see," Clara impatiently asked as she tugged on Dad's arm.

"Just one second, I'm trying to find where it is," he answered as he scanned the sky, directed by the arrows in the app.

"Ah-ha, there it is!" Dad exclaimed as he finally found it.

"Where? Where?" both Clara and Isaac asked.

"Okay kids, look over there," Dad said as he pointed towards the horizon in the direction of the constellation. He lowered the phone to their height so they could help see what to look for.

After a pause as both kids tried to find it, Clara shouted out, "I see it! I see it!"

"I don't. Where?" Isaac dejectedly said.

Dad tried to point it out to him but he was a little too young to figure out what stars to look for.

Clara was so excited. "I bet unicorns live on those stars," she declared.

"Well honey, they wouldn't live on the stars. Those stars are like our Sun. They are flaming balls of fire – it would be too hot for a unicorn," Dad explained.

"Well where did the astronaut say they could live then?" Clara asked.

"On planets, baby," Dad answered. Planets travel around stars just like our planet travels around the sun. There could be lots of planets that circle those stars. That's where the unicorns could live."

"Ooohhh…," Clara said, as if she was still trying to process all of that. She went on, "Oh unicorns, I love you!"

"Alright kids, it's late, we better get in to bed before your mother gets mad at us. Take one last look and let's get back inside."

Dad scooped up Isaac and carried him back as Clara lingered, longingly looking up at the night sky, dreaming and wishing to someday see a unicorn.

The next morning, Clara bolted out of bed early. It was show-and-tell day at school and she knew just what she wanted to share. She drew a picture and carefully placed it in a folder in her backpack to bring to school.

That morning at school, Clara told her class about the astronaut show during her turn at show-and-tell. Her teacher excitedly asked, "Wait, that was you? I saw that too! I was going to tell you that I heard a question from another girl named Clara who loved unicorns... but I didn't realize it was you!"

The kids in her class thought that that was pretty cool. Clara also told them how she had seen the unicorn constellation that the astronauts had referred to. She got out the picture she had drawn of the constellation and proudly showed it off.

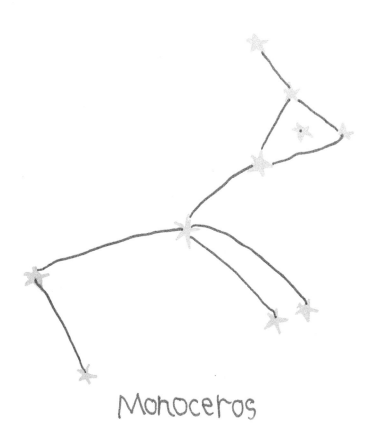

Monoceros

The other kids in her class expressed that they couldn't wait to try to see it themselves that night. They were all buzzing about unicorns and astronauts and stars.

It was an unseasonably warm day, so after school let out, Mom took Clara and her siblings on a walk around a nearby lake. There was a wooded path around the lake where they would frequently spot wildlife and loved to find sticks and explore.

Usually Clara and Isaac went exploring together, but today, Isaac was feeling tired and hung back with Mom. Clara skipped ahead, looking for a stick to walk with and imagining that she was hiking in an enchanted forest filled with unicorns.

"Clara, don't get too far ahead," her mom warned.

"I know," Clara responded, hardly giving it a second thought.

As she aimlessly swung around trees, hopped over logs, and swung her stick at leaves, she meandered a little off the beaten path. All of a sudden, she heard a twig snap. Her heart leapt. *What was that?* she thought. Out of curiosity, she headed towards where the sound had come from.

At first, she didn't see anything, but she heard another sound and so continued to creep forward trying to locate the source of the noise. There was some thick brush blocking the way. She searched for a way around, and finally spotted a small opening big enough for her to crawl through.

She got down on her hands and knees and began to crawl. But she didn't even make it through before she spotted something that made her freeze in her tracks.

What she saw next would change Clara's life forever.

Chapter 5

In front of her was a small clearing. Right in the middle was a sight she had only ever dreamed of. A ray of sunlight glistened off the most beautiful, sparkly thing she had ever seen. *Could it be?* She thought. *Was this a dream?*

She blinked. It was still there. In front of her stood what could only be described as a real-life unicorn. It blinked. Clara gasped. She could only manage a whisper, "Are you a… unicorn?"

If Clara didn't love unicorns so much, what happened next would have caused her to faint. The animal in front of her could talk! It answered in a sweet, soft voice, "You must be Clara. And yes, I am what you call a unicorn!"

"How... how do you know my name?" Clara stammered.

It wasn't her imagination. The unicorn went on, "Never mind that now, I'll tell you all about how I found you later. You can really see me?"

"Yes! Yes! I can!" Clara excitedly answered. "Your horn is sparkly and your mane is so beautiful - I see pinks and purples and greens and gold!"

"Finally! Oh, I'm just so excited!" the unicorn exclaimed as it did a little hop of joy.

"What's your name?" Clara asked.

"Well I don't have a name yet, at least in your language," the unicorn responded.

"What should I call you then?" Clara wondered aloud. "Your horn is the sparkliest thing I have seen – even more than glitter," she observed. "What about glitter… glitter something. Hmmm… How about glitter… star?" she said, inspired by the unicorn constellation she had just learned about. "Yeah, how about Glitterstar?"

"Glitterstar?" The unicorn repeated, trying it out. "Glitterstar! I love it!"

Clara beamed a huge smile as she ran up to Glitterstar and gave her a big hug.

Just then, the magical moment was interrupted with the sound of Clara's mom calling out, "Claaarrraa! Clara, where are you?"

"Over here, Mom!" Clara responded, still hugging Glitterstar.

"Come back to the path," Mom yelled back.

Clara turned to Glitterstar and asked, "Do you want to come with me? You can meet my mom and brother!"

Glitterstar leapt for joy again and responded in an excited voice, "Yes, yes I would love to come with you!" She paused though and her smile turned down slightly as she went on, "But I need to warn you, they won't be able to see me. Only true believers can see a unicorn. And even then, we usually only reveal ourselves to one special person here on Earth."

"Oh…" Clara responded, not quite sure what to say. "And I am your special person?"

"Yes, yes you are! And because you are a true believer, you were able to see me!" Glitterstar explained.

"Let's go anyways," Clara urged. Clara practically bounded through the woods on her way back to the path, giggling the whole way with Glitterstar at her side.

Soon they found the path and approached Mom. Mom inquired, "Were you talking to someone, Clara?"

"Yes, my new unicorn friend, Glitterstar!" Clara exclaimed.

"Well, stay with us on the path, honey," Mom responded, assuming that Clara must just be playing pretend.

Clara looked at Mom, and then back to Glitterstar, and back again. She couldn't believe that Mom was just acting normal. *She really must not be able to see Glitterstar*, she thought.

Clara spent the rest of the walk around the lake in silence with Glitterstar at her side. A permanent smile stretched across Clara's face. Her dream had come true. She still could not believe it. Her eyes darted back and forth between watching out for roots and rocks ahead of her, and glancing to her side to catch a glimpse of Glitterstar.

Looking at Glitterstar was almost as if seeing color for the first time. In comparison, the rest of the world looked black and white. These colors were more vibrant than any Clara had ever seen. Her coat was a bright white that seemed to glisten in the sunlight. Her mane seemed to float as she pranced, almost as if it were not held down by the same rules of gravity as her own hair. Her mane and tail were so colorful. She spotted pastel purples, pinks, mint green, and even gold. Clara couldn't

47

quite put a name to the colors. They seemed to change with every slight movement. Perhaps they were new colors that she had never seen before. Glitter-looking sparkles seemed to illuminate from within. Unlike normal sparkles that reflected light, these seemed to sparkle even in the shade.

The color of Glitterstar's eyes nearly took her breath away. They were a lavender purple, she noticed. But it was a purple more vivid than any purple she had ever seen. They seemed to glow from within, not simply reflect the light.

Her hooves matched her eyes, but without the glow. Instead, they appeared polished and smooth. Dirt and dust did not seem to stick to them as she trudged along the path.

And last but not least there was the horn, the signature of a unicorn. It was a shade of gold, but like a diamond, its sparkle completely overwhelmed any sense of color. Light danced off her spiraled horn with such brilliance that the forest floor seemed to be illuminated. It reminded her of the way light sparkles off a calm lake as the sun rises early in the morning. She wondered if Glitterstar's horn might actually have thousands of tiny diamonds embedded in it. It radiated a glitter and sparkle that would make a jewelry-adorned queen envious.

When they arrived back at their house, Clara said, "Mom, I'm going to go play in the backyard for a bit, alright?"

Mom answered, "Sure sweetie."

Clara whispered to Glitterstar, "Come with me."

"What was that?" Mom asked, thinking Clara was talking to her.

"Oh, nothing Mommy," Clara responded.

Clara giggled as she and Glitterstar bounded around the side of the house and into the backyard.

Clara was almost bursting. She had so many questions for Glitterstar and things to tell her and talk about. As soon as she was sure they were out of earshot, she burst out in rapid fire succession, "You are so beautiful! Where did you come from? How did you find me? Can you stay? Where will you sleep? Are you hungr—"

Glitterstar was laughing at this barrage of questions and cut her off with, "Clara, Clara, calm down! I am here to stay. Relax, don't worry!"

"I just have so much to ask you!" Clara responded.

Glitterstar chuckled, "I know! I am excited too! I have been looking for a human friend for a long time. There are not many true believers anymore."

"How did you find me?" Clara asked.

Glitterstar explained, "Well, I have been searching for a while for a girl who truly believed in unicorns. And then one night I was scanning television channels and I—"

"Wait, how do you watch television? Do you have a TV?" Clara interrupted.

"Oh, well my horn acts as an antenna," Glitterstar responded. "I can see the images in my head!"

"Cool!" Clara exclaimed.

"So, I was scanning television channels," Glitterstar continued, "when I came across a program from astronauts streaming from space. I stopped to watch because space reminded me of home, when all of sudden the astronaut read a letter from a girl asking about unicorns in space."

"That was me!" Clara chimed in.

Glitterstar continued, "I just couldn't believe it. I knew that that girl must be a true believer. I set out at once, that very night, to come searching for you."

"How did you know where I lived?" Clara asked.

"I replayed what I had seen in my mind over and over," Glitterstar explained. "And I noticed a faint indentation on the letter. Whoever wrote the return address must have done so after the letter was already in the envelope. It left an indentation on the paper."

"My mom wrote it!" Clara excitedly confirmed. "The envelope was already sealed at that point."

"I was just barely able to make out your city and street," Glitterstar continued. "I wasn't exactly sure where you lived, but I didn't care. I now knew that there was a girl out there who believed in unicorns and so I set out determined to find you!"

"Oh, I am so glad you did," Clara replied as she gave Glitterstar a big hug. "How did you end up finding me?"

"I walked up and down your street for days, listening for anyone to utter the name 'Clara'. At first, I was worried about finding too many girls with the name 'Clara' and trying to determine which girl it had been. But as I searched, I realized that there are not many girls with that name around here. And then I started to get discouraged. I couldn't find a 'Clara' anywhere. I came to these trees to take a nap, and had just settled in, when all of a sudden I heard someone call out 'Clara'!"

"That was my mom!" Clara added.

"I couldn't believe it. I was so excited; I froze in place. I was so nervous. I couldn't believe that I might have actually found you."

Clara giggled, "Well actually, it was kind of *me* who found *you*!"

"Right you are!" Glitterstar responded. "To think, after all these years of looking for a true believer, it was a true believer who found me!"

"Claaarrraa!" Mom shouted from out the back door. "Time to come in for dinner!"

"Just a second, Mom!" Clara called back.

"Will you be okay? I don't want to leave you out here," Clara said as she squeezed Glitterstar.

"You go along. I'll be more than fine. This is the best day of my life," Glitterstar responded.

"This is the best day of *my* life too," agreed Clara. "I don't want to leave you, ever."

"Go ahead," Glitterstar urged. "I'm never going to leave you. I'll be right out here. We have our whole life ahead of us. But right now, you have to eat!"

Clara gave her one last giant hug and then skipped up the hill to her house, looking back over her shoulder every few steps.

By the time she had finished dinner, it was starting to get dark. Her mom would not let her go back outside. Clara peered out the window and could see Glitterstar curled up, resting in the backyard with a smile on her face. Clara smiled back and then decided that she would try to color a picture of Glitterstar.

Clara pulled her chair up to the window, grabbed a blank sheet of paper and a book to use as support, and started to draw and color. Her markers couldn't quite capture the brilliance that she saw. The colors just weren't anywhere near as rich and magical. But she did her best.

"Mom, how do you spell Glitterstar?" she called out.

"G – L – I – T – T – E – R – S – T – A – R," Mom called out slowly as Clara wrote across the page.

After Clara had finished, she went to proudly show off her picture to Mom.

"This is Glitterstar, my new friend!" Clara declared.

"Wow honey!" Mom exclaimed, "I think that is your most beautiful unicorn picture yet!"

"That's because Glitterstar *is* the most beautiful unicorn *ever*," Clara matter-of-factly responded.

Glitterstar

That evening, Clara looked out the window every chance that she got. Each time, she held her breath as she peered outside, half expecting Glitterstar to be gone. But she was still there. That evening Clara fell asleep with a giant smile on her face, happier than she had ever been before.

When Clara awoke the next morning, she lay in her bed a moment. All of a sudden, she remembered. *Glitterstar,* she thought, as she bolted upright in her bed. She scampered down the ladder of her bunk bed and flung open the shades.

"Too bright! Too bright!" Isaac cried out as the sunlight rushed across the darkened room. He buried his head under the covers to hide from the light.

Clara's eyes adjusted to the brightness. She peered outside. Her heart sank. She frantically scanned her entire backyard. But she could not see Glitterstar anywhere.

Chapter 6

Tears started to swell in Clara's eyes. Had it all just been a dream? It seemed too real. It had to be real. She frantically searched her mind, trying to separate what had actually happened yesterday from what had happened in her dreams last night.

Then she remembered. *The picture*, she thought. *I had drawn a picture!* She rushed out of her bedroom, scampered down the hall, pounded her feet quickly down the stairs, and searched for where she had left the picture. *If it was just a dream,* she thought, *then I won't be able to find the picture I had drawn of Glitterstar!*

Tears were swelling up, clouding her vision. The picture wasn't on the table. It wasn't on the kitchen counter. She was starting to have trouble seeing due to her tears. Just then, out of the corner of her eye, she spotted it.

"My picture!" she exclaimed out loud. The picture was stuck to the front of the refrigerator, held up by a magnet. *Mom must have hung it up,* she thought. *And if there is a picture, Glitterstar must be real!*

She wiped away the tears from her eyes. No sooner had the first worry disappeared from her mind, then a second one swiftly replaced it. *But where did she go?* she thought. *What had happened to Glitterstar?*

"Clara, get ready for school!" Mom called. Clara reluctantly headed back upstairs to get dressed and ready for the school day. She did her best to hold back tears. Mom noticed her sulking around and asked, "Clara, what's wrong sweetie? You look so sad."

Clara explained, "Glitterstar is gone, Mommy. I can't find her anywhere."

Mom, thinking that Clara must be referring to one of her many unicorn toys, replied, "Clara, that's why you need to put your things away. Clean up after school and I'm sure you will find it. We need to get going to school now though. You're going to be late!"

Clara, remembering that her mom could not see Glitterstar, decided not to correct her. *Maybe Glitterstar would turn up after school,* she thought. The thought gave her some hope and cheered her up, just a little.

After having a yogurt cup for breakfast and getting everything ready for school, Clara grabbed her backpack and went out the front door to head to the van.

No sooner had she opened the front door than she screeched in delight. There, sitting on the front steps, was Glitterstar!

"Glitterstar!" she called out as she threw open the door and ran to give her a big hug. "I thought you were gone! I couldn't find you anywhere!"

"I didn't want to miss you before you headed off to school," explained Glitterstar. "I woke up in the middle of the night and realized that I might sleep in and miss you. So, I moved to the front steps to be sure that didn't happen."

"Oh Glitterstar," Clara lovingly scolded. "You scared me so much."

"I'm sorry, I didn't mean to scare—" Glitterstar started to apologize before interrupting herself as she remembered something. "Oh, I almost forgot! Here, I made this for you," she said as she scooped up a flower wreath and gently placed it on Clara's head.

"You made this for me?" Clara exclaimed. "I just love it. It's so beautiful!"

In all the excitement, Clara had almost forgotten about all of the questions she had been thinking about last night that she had not yet asked Glitterstar. "Glitterstar," she inquired, "I never asked, where did you come from?"

"Well, it's a long story," Glitterstar started. "Actually, you kind of already know."

"I do?" Clara asked, puzzled.

"Well, yes, your letter to the astronauts!" Glitterstar explained. "You thought that unicorns must live on a different planet in outer space. And you were right, we are from a distant planet!"

"I knew it! I knew it!" Clara gleefully exclaimed.

"It's a very long story for another time, but I was born on a planet very far away. One of many planets where unicorns live," Glitterstar added.

"There's more than one planet of unicorns?" Clara excitedly asked.

"Yes, yes," Glitterstar confirmed. "But years ago, I travelled to Earth with my parents and many of our friends."

"Why did you come here?" Clara asked.

Glitterstar started to explain further, "Well, when I was young, the—"

At that moment, Isaac burst out the door carrying his backpack on his back. Their mom followed, carrying Emma in her car seat.

"Come on, Clara, get in the car or we are going to be late!" Mom urged as she hoisted Emma and her car seat into the van.

"You'll have to tell me more another time," Clara whispered to Glitterstar. "Can you come with me to school?"

"Sure! I'll follow you there!" Glitterstar exclaimed. But she quickly added, "Though you can't get distracted from learning!"

"Yippee!" Clara squealed. "I won't! I won't! I promise!"

"I'll follow you there. Go ahead and get in the van!" Glitterstar said.

Clara bounded over to the van and hopped into the open door. She buckled her seatbelt and her mom closed the door and started off to school. Clara craned her neck to look out the back window to make sure that Glitterstar was following. Sure enough, there she was, prancing along behind them.

Before long, they arrived at school and Clara said goodbye to her mom as she raced out of the van. Glitterstar was waiting for her by the steps of the school.

Clara was amazed at how fast Glitterstar could gallop. "Wow, you aren't even out of breath!" Clara observed.

"That was just a nice little jog for me!" Glitterstar responded. "You go into school now before the bell rings."

"What are you going to do?" Clara asked.

Glitterstar nodded towards the playground and explained, "I'll wait by the playground for when you come out for recess. Now go learn a lot!"

Clara gave Glitterstar one last big hug before scampering up the stairs into school and towards her classroom. Moments after she entered the room, the bell rang out, signaling the start of class.

"Gooooooood morning Eagle Nation!" the school's principal cheerily greeted the students over the loudspeaker. Clara didn't hear the rest of what he said as she drifted off into a daydream about Glitterstar.

The rest of the morning seemed to take forever. She couldn't wait for recess to see Glitterstar again. But she also couldn't wait for lunch to tell her friends that she had found a real unicorn!

After a morning of math, reading, and social studies, the bell rang out and her teacher said, "Alright class, it's time for lunch!" Clara practically jumped out of her seat, hurried to her locker, found her lunch box, and headed down to the lunchroom.

She found her usual table and slid into a seat between her two best friends, Grace and Penny. "Clara!" her friend exclaimed, leaning over and giving Clara a big hug. Clara squeezed her back and then responded, "You are *never* going to believe what I found yesterday!"

"A real-life fairy?" Penny asked.

"Nope, even better than a fairy!" Clara responded as she cracked open her usual unicorn lunchbox to see what her mom had packed for lunch.

"A mermaid?" Grace guessed.

"Is it your pretty wreath?" Penny asked, noticing the wreath that Clara was wearing that Glitterstar had given her that morning.

"Well, not really, but kind of..." Clara tried to explain.

69

"Oh, just tell us, just tell us!" Penny pleaded.

"A real-life unicorn!" Clara burst out, hardly able to contain it this long.

"A unicorn?" both Grace and Penny repeated in unison.

"Uh huh, and her name is Glitterstar, well, I gave her that name actually, and she is the most beautiful unicorn I have ever seen, well in pictures I mean, because she is the only unicorn I have ever seen," Clara giggled, talking as fast as she could out of sheer excitement.

"Oooo, what color is her mane?" Grace asked.

Clara responded, "it's like pink and purple and more, I can't explain it, but it's just so beautiful and—"

"Where is she now?" Penny interrupted.

"She's outside waiting for me," Clara answered. "Maybe she will come play with us at recess!"

The girls excitedly chatted some more as they also quickly ate their sandwiches and fruit so they could be done as soon as the recess bell sounded.

"Bah-ringgggggggg" the bell sounded. All three girls practically leapt up at the same time, dropping their lunch boxes in a bin before heading out of the lunchroom and down the hall to the playground outside.

As they skipped down the hallway side by side holding hands, Clara cautioned, "Now I don't know if you will be able to see her. Not everyone can see her. Actually, so far, I only know that I can. She said only 'true believers' can see unicorns."

"We are true believers!" Grace insisted as they pushed open the door and went outside. Penny nodded in agreement.

And there, lying peacefully in the corner of the playground, was Glitterstar. Clara shrieked in delight and bolted across the playground towards her.

Grace and Penny awkwardly exchanged glances. Neither wanted to confess that they couldn't see what Clara was running towards, nor any sign of a unicorn. That would mean they were not true believers, so they said nothing and both quickly followed Clara, although a bit cautious and unsure of what to do or say.

Clara noticed her friends approach and called out to them, "See, don't you see her? This is Glitterstar!"

Both girls stood there speechless for a moment. "Uhh…" started Grace.

"Well…" followed Penny.

Clara was confused as she thought, *why were they so speechless? Were they star-struck in front of a real-life unicorn?*

But then it hit her. *Oh no, maybe they couldn't see Glitterstar either!*

Chapter 7

Glitterstar immediately recognized the look of dismay on Clara's face. "Clara," she began, "remember what I told you about how long it took for me to find a true believer?"

Clara nodded as tears began swelling in her eyes.

"Well," Glitterstar continued. "So many girls *think* they believe in unicorns. But deep down, they have their doubts. All it takes is the tiniest, slightest thought that unicorns might just be a fairy tale. Or an imaginary friend. It is rare for someone to have such conviction as you. To truly believe that unicorns are actually, truly real."

"But... But..." stammered Clara as a tear began rolling down her cheek. "But they are my best friends."

Glitterstar nuzzled her cheek. "I know, honey. Maybe in time you will be able to help them see that unicorns are real. But it may take time. Don't get discouraged."

This cheered Clara up. Always the optimist, she realized that she could help them believe. She thought to herself, *I'll be able to do it... and then they will be able to see her too!*

Her friends, still slightly embarrassed, had retreated to the monkey bars. "Clara," called out Grace. "Come play with us on the monkey bars!"

Clara gave one last squeeze to Glitterstar and bounded over to the monkey bars. She joined her friends swinging from arm to arm to the other side of the platform.

As they were swinging back and forth, a younger class of kids came out for their recess too. The littler kids swarmed the playground, scampering up the ladders and stairs, swooshing down slides, and chasing one another around in a game of tag.

Clara moved to the bar that the girls used for doing flips and hanging upside down on. She wrapped the bar with her legs and arms and called out to her friends, "Look, I'm a koala!"

Her friends giggled. Grace went next and hung upside down by her feet, swinging back and forth.

Clara barely noticed the littler kids running around playing tag. She was used to it, so hardly gave it a second thought. A little girl named Mia whooshed right by her as she barely dodged the outstretched arm of a little boy whose name Clara couldn't remember.

Mia rushed around the outside of the slides with the boy hot on her heels. She faked a cut right, and then turned sharply left to the base of the stairs ascending up to the slides and bridge. Her move threw off the boy just long enough for Mia to bound a couple of stairs up without getting tagged. The boy quickly recovered from the fake out and began ascending the stairs too.

This particular playground had platforms that must have been over fifteen feet high, much higher than the typical ones found at most playgrounds.

As soon as Mia reached the top, she bounded across the bridge towards a set of slides down which she hoped to make her escape. The only problem was that other children were already lined up waiting their turn to go down them. And others were just hanging around and chatting. Mia started to squeeze between and around them, trying to budge her way to the front so she could make her escape. She saw a path around some kids on the edge of the platform that looked like it would take her directly to the mouth of one of the slides.

She quickly cut around them. But as she shuffled along the edge, a kid took a step backwards, not noticing that Mia was behind him. Her left shoe just barely snagged the kid's heel. Mia lost her balance and let out a shriek as she tumbled sideways.

While most of the highest platform was surrounded by safety railings, this particular area was left open for kids to climb up from the ladder below.

Mia stretched out her arm desperately trying to grab ahold of the top ladder wrung, but her fingers couldn't quite reach. Before she knew it, she was in free fall from fifteen feet high. Her shriek turned to an outright scream.

Chapter 8

Out of the corner of her eye, Clara had caught a flash. It was Mia edging along the outside of the platform. She glanced up at the very moment that Mia tumbled off. Out of pure instinct, Clara lunged forward towards the falling girl.

As this was happening, two teachers were chatting with each other along the fence of the playground while keeping an eye on the students. One was Clara's teacher, while the other was the gym teacher. They heard Mia's shriek and looked up also just in time to see her tumble off the edge.

Time seemed to slow down. The teachers looked on in horror as Mia dropped closer and closer to the ground. They could see Clara dashing towards her but there was no way she could make it in time. And even if she did, what would happen? Would she even be able to break Mia's fall?

Clara moved her legs with all her might. She stretched out her arms towards the falling girl. But her legs couldn't move fast enough. She wasn't going to make it.

Just then, she felt a strong push from behind. Glitterstar had dashed into action and was shoving Clara forward with her head while lifting her up off the ground. Clara, lifted by Glitterstar, reached Mia and quickly wrapped her outstretched arms around her. Clara twisted her body to turn Mia up and get herself underneath in order to break Mia's impact with the ground. Clara braced for a hard impact herself.

But the hard impact never came. Glitterstar caught Clara with her outstretched legs and almost imperceptibly slowed her fall the last foot to gently set them down on the ground.

The teachers stood there, frozen in disbelief at how Clara had been able to catch Mia. They hadn't been able to see Glitterstar, of course, so to them it looked like an unbelievable diving catch by Clara. A second later, they snapped out of their shock and rushed quickly towards the girls.

Mia was shaken up, but completely unharmed. Clara's catch had been so gentle that Mia did not even have a scrape or bruise, thanks to Glitterstar's assist. Clara, who had acted out of instinct, was only beginning to realize what she had done.

"Mia, Mia, are you alright?" Clara's teacher desperately questioned.

"Uh, yes, I think. Clara caught me!" she responded as she sat up, herself still processing what had just happened.

"Are you hurt anywhere?" the gym teacher asked.

Mia moved her arms and legs, searching for a scrape or bruise, but found no such injury.

All of sudden the teachers realized that Clara must have taken the brunt of the fall on Mia's behalf. Their concern shifted as they turned to Clara and the gym teacher asked, "Clara, are you hurt?"

Clara was still a little stunned at what had happened, but she composed herself. After quickly assessing her situation, she answered, "No, I think I'm alright."

"Clara, that was amazing!" Clara's teacher exclaimed. "Mia could have been badly hurt. You saved her!"

Clara blushed. Mia leaned over and gave Clara a big hug. But then Clara remembered the help she had from Glitterstar and wanted to make sure that she didn't take all of the credit. "Well, my unicorn helped give me the extra nudge I needed," Clara replied. "And she made sure we didn't smack into the ground," she added.

"Well I am sure glad that you had that unicorn's help. You are a hero, Clara!" her teacher replied. She was playing along with what she assumed was Clara's imaginary friend.

The other kids, who had fallen silent at the sight of the fall, started all talking at once about what they had just witnessed. Those who had missed it were asking what had happened, while those who had seen it were trying to explain.

"Clara is a hero," one kid said.

"She caught that girl," another explained.

"I can't believe what I just saw," yet another commented.

Clara's teacher led both girls off the playground and into the school to the nurse's office to be checked over to ensure they didn't have any hidden injuries.

The gym teacher stood watching the kids excitedly chat, lost in his own thoughts. Besides being the gym teacher, he was also the soccer coach for the school. *Wow*, he thought. *I've never seen anyone move that fast or jump that far before. I've got to get Clara to join the soccer team!*

Before long, the entire school was talking about what had happened. Normally, things like this grow as they spread until they become fantastical and inflated. But in this case, what had originally happened was already beyond belief, at least from the perspective of non-unicorn believers. No exaggeration was needed. And everybody who had seen it could report, Clara lunged faster and farther than anyone thought possible, all while catching a falling girl without either girl getting a scratch. "It was almost as if they landed on a pillow," the kids said.

Of course, it didn't take long before the principal had also heard of the near miss and heroic action. He called an all-school assembly to address the students at the very end of the day.

As each class filed into the gym and took their seats in the bleachers or floor, everyone was excitedly chatting about the same thing.

After everyone had found their seats, the principal turned on the microphone and urged the students, and even the teachers, to hush.

"Students. Students! Listen up, school will be over soon but we have something important to talk about first," he urged.

The students slowly drifted off from their excited conversations as a hush fell over the room.

"I'm sure all of you have guessed why I've gathered you together today," he started. "Earlier today while some of the classes were at recess, we had something frightening and wonderful happen."

Children exchanged knowing glances, for they knew what this was about.

"One of our students tripped and fell off of the high playground platform. One of our other students saw this happen and was able to catch her. Both students are completely fine, thankfully!"

Some students clapped at this, but the principal continued on. "This situation underscores the importance of safety while on the playground. Even though nobody was hurt, in all likelihood it could have ended much worse. The student could have ended up breaking a bone or having serious head trauma, likely ending up in the hospital."

The students all had a glum look on their face as the gravity of the situation started to sink in.

The principal went on, "Now it isn't anybody's fault and nobody is to blame. But we are going to be instituting a new rule that no tag is allowed on playground equipment. Rushing around on platforms high up creates an unsafe situation. And we might not always be so fortunate to have a hero save the day."

The students looked at each other disappointed, for they never liked new rules that restricted their play. But they understood.

"Speaking of heroes," the principal said as he motioned towards another teacher to bring something out. "I have an exciting announcement and award to hand out today."

Chapter 9

The children started chattering with each other, speculating what the award could be.

"While we had a very close call today, we also have a hero to celebrate," the principal explained. "When the student stumbled off the platform, another of our students didn't hesitate for a second and lunged to catch that student. This student didn't think twice about trying to help, even though she faced the real possibility of injury herself. Her quick thinking and selfless act saved the day."

As they listened, students started looking around the room, seeking out Clara, the girl they had heard about. Slowly, all eyes settled on her.

The principal held up a medal for all to see. "I have a very special medal here. At the beginning of the year we decided to institute a new peacebuilder award. We wanted this to be the top award for a student who did something extraordinary to build the peace in our school. As chance would have it, the medal just arrived last week."

He looked down at the medal and read the inscription aloud, "It says, 'Peacebuilder Hero Award'. I wasn't sure yet exactly what type of action would merit this medal. But as soon as I heard about what had happened today, I instantly knew that this girl was deserving of it. And now, can we have a drumroll please."

The students started drumming the bleachers excitedly.

"The first ever Peacebuilder Hero Award goes to... Clara!" the principal proudly announced. "Clara, come on up!"

Clara was blushing bright red. She made her way up to the front. Several students started to clap, which contagiously spread through the audience until the entire room was clapping for her. As she reached the front, the principal shook her hand and hung the medal around her neck.

He turned back to the students as they quieted down and said, "As the student fell, Clara lunged as fast as she could towards her. She dove and caught the student in her arms and somehow broke her fall, without getting hurt herself, to save both from harm. If she had hesitated even a fraction of a second, it would have been too late. Her natural, selfless reaction saved the day. Let's hear it for Clara, our Peacebuilder Hero!"

Once again, the gym burst out in loud applause. The applause continued straight through the last bell of the day, which could hardly be heard. As the applause quieted down, the principal had to announce, "And with that, have a great afternoon students, school is dismissed for the day!"

Several teachers came up to Clara and congratulated her, thanking her for her heroic actions. The gym teacher caught Clara before she left and pulled her aside.

"I saw what you did today," he began. "It was truly amazing. We could really use someone with such quick reflexes on our soccer team. I've never seen someone move so fast. Have you ever been interested in joining the soccer team?"

"Well, I don't know." Clara cautiously replied. "I don't really know how to play. And it wasn't just me, I had help from my unicorn, you know."

The gym teacher wasn't fazed. He was used to hearing about unicorns from his students. "Your unicorn can play too!" he replied, hoping to entice her.

"Hmmm," Clara said as she thought out loud. "Well, in that case, as long as she can play too, I guess so. I'll have to ask my mom though."

The gym teacher was getting excited. "Yes, yes, talk to her. I'll call her too and let her know when the practices and games are."

"I should get going now," Clara responded.

94

"Of course, you've had a very eventful day. Congratulations, way to go!" he said with a big smile on his face as he held out his hand to give her a high five.

Clara reached up and smacked his hand, a little unsure about soccer but feeling proud that he had asked her. She quickly bounded up the stairs back to her classroom to get her backpack and then meet her mom and Glitterstar outside.

Later that evening at dinner, Dad asked about Clara's day, and she proudly recounted the story of how she had saved the girl and was awarded a medal. She handed him the medal from around her neck so he could see it for himself.

Dad beamed with pride, "Clara, baby, I am so proud of you! Way to go!"

Clara, never wanting to take full credit, responded, "But Daddy, Glitterstar helped.

Without her I wouldn't have made it in time."

"Yes, and way to go Glitterstar!" her Dad added. "I know what we need to do, we need to celebrate! Let's have some ice cream for dessert!"

"Yippee!" Isaac called out.

"Oh, I almost forgot," Mom interjected. "I got a call today from your gym teacher, Clara. He thinks you would be a great addition to the soccer team. What do you think, sweetie?"

"Well, as long as Glitterstar can play too, I think I'll give it a try," Clara replied.

"Clara, that's great," Dad added. "Not only did you receive a medal but you got recruited for the soccer team on the same day. Two things to celebrate!"

The children quickly scarfed down the rest of their meal in anticipation of ice cream.

"Oh, that reminds me," Dad said as he remembered something else that he was going to tell the kids. "I thought we could go camping this weekend. We can go hiking and sleep in a tent and make s'mores. What do you think?"

"Yes!" replied Clara. "Can we bring our sleeping bags?" she asked.

"Of course!" Mom replied.

"Ohhh, I can't wait!" Clara squealed with excitement, until she remembered Glitterstar. "But Daddy, can Glitterstar come with? Pretty pllll-eeeeaasssssseeee," she begged.

"Well, I don't see why not. After all, she did help save the day!" Dad chuckled.

"Yippee!" Clara exclaimed.

And with a twinkle in his eye, Dad added, "And you never know — a unicorn just might come in handy in the woods!"

With that, Dad got up from the table, brought out Clara's favorite flavor of ice cream, and dished out big scoops for all.

The End

Don't Miss the Next Glitterstar Adventures!

2 Continue the series where Book 1 left off! Join Clara and Glitterstar on their camping trip to the woods for the weekend. What was supposed to be an uneventful weekend in the wilderness ends up being a whole new adventure!

3 In Book 3, Clara and Glitterstar accept the gym teacher's offer to join the soccer team. Can they learn the game and work together to help their team win their way to a championship for the first time in their school's history?

Made in the USA
Monee, IL
18 September 2022